This book
belongs to:

· · · · · · · · · · · · · · ·

SIMON SPOTLIGHT
An imprint of Simon & Schuster Children's Publishing Division
1230 Avenue of the Americas
New York, New York 10020

Adapted from the nonfiction segments entitled "Imagine That," "How To Be Safe,"
and "How It Works" from the animated television series *The Busy World
of Richard Scarry*™, produced by Paramount Pictures and Cinar.

Designed and produced by Les Livres du Dragon d'Or

Printed in Italy

10 9 8 7 6 5 4 3 2 1

Library of Congress Catalog Card Number: 97-65737

ISBN: 0-689-81631-6

Dinosaurs and Other Fun Things

Recycling
Dinosaurs
Mines
Icebergs

Simon Spotlight

RECYCLING

We all throw away lots of garbage. But much of it can be reused.
This is called recycling!

It's time to take out the garbage.
"Umpff!" complains Huckle. "This is heavy!"
"It is amazing how much garbage we throw away," Lowly says.

"What are you doing with all this stuff, boys?" Mr. Fixit asks.

"It's garbage. We're throwing it away," Huckle replies.

"Don't just throw it away. You can recycle some of it," Mr. Fixit says.
"What's recycling?" the boys ask.
"Recycling means using things over and over again," Mr. Fixit explains.
"First, separate paper, glass, plastic, and cans. Each has its own recycling bin."

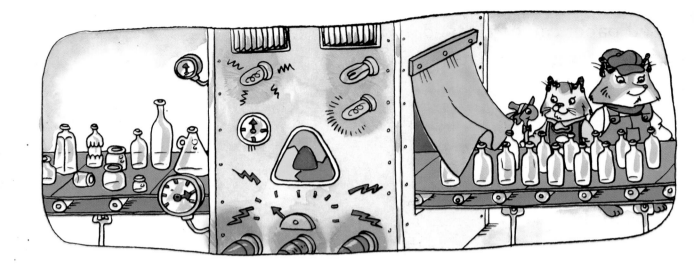

"Old glass jars and bottles can be made into new ones," Mr. Fixit says. "That sounds like magic!" Lowly says.

"Plastic containers and wrappers can be turned into binders or rulers," Mr. Fixit continues.

"This is great!" Huckle exclaims. "Look at all the things you can make."

"Used paper can be cleaned and reused to make greeting cards and writing paper," says Mr. Fixit.

"Come on, Lowly," Huckle says. "Let's find more things to recycle!"

"I'm on my way!"

DINOSAURS

Millions of years ago, before people lived on Earth, our planet was inhabited by creatures called dinosaurs. Let's learn about them!

At the library, Huckle and Lowly have found some interesting books.
"Yikes!" Lowly exclaims.
"Look at this bird, Huckle."

"Don't worry, Lowly," Huckle says.
"That bird is a dinosaur who lived on Earth a long, long time ago!"

"Dinosaurs were reptiles, which means their blood was cold," Huckle explains. "Some of them might have been covered with scales or plates. Others might have had hair or fur."
"What strange-looking creatures they were!" Lowly says.

"Some dinosaurs were very small while others were taller than trees! Many dined on plants and leaves," Huckle says.
"Ha, ha! A dining dinosaur!" laughs Lowly.

"Some dinosaurs were dangerous," Huckle continues. "They would scare all the others."

"Gee," says Lowly, "I get goosebumps just looking at their pictures!"

"Dinosaurs disappeared from the earth. No one is sure why," Huckle says.

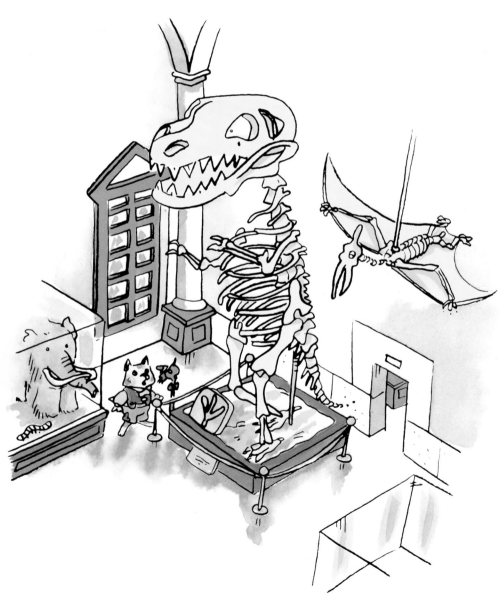

"But we can learn about them from skeletons and fossils found in the ground. These are kept in museums so everyone can see them."

MINES

Have you ever wondered where shiny metal and sparkling jewels come from? Both are found deep inside the earth in mines. Would you like to learn about them?

Huckle and Lowly admire the window of a jewelry shop.

"Why don't we ever find jewels around here in Busytown?" asks Huckle.

"Because jewels have to be dug from mines, Huckle," Lowly says.

Mines are tunnels carved into mountains or dug deep under the ground. Workers called miners spend their day working in these tunnels.

Things of great worth, such as gold, silver, and precious stones, can be found in mines. Minerals and coal are also found there. Miners dig with picks and shovels. They use powerful explosives, too.

BOOM!

After the explosion, miners may find gold or other kinds of metal.
Their precious discoveries are brought to the surface by a special train.

Then, when cut and polished, the gold and gems will find their way to the jewelry shop.

"Do you think there may be jewels under Busytown, Lowly?" Huckle asks.

"Let's start digging and find out!" says Lowly.

ICEBERGS

In the cold seas that surround the North and South Poles, you can see floating mountains of ice, called icebergs. Here is how they are made!

Huckle and Lowly are traveling by ship through cold Arctic waters.

"Look! An iceberg!"
Huckle points.
"I wonder how it got
here?"

Icebergs come from
glaciers. In some places,
it is so cold that snow
never melts. It gets
higher and higher and
becomes very hard.
Over millions of years, it
turns to ice, and becomes
a glacier.

Icebergs are big chunks of ice that have broken off a glacier.

The sound of ice breaking from a glacier is as loud as thunder. CRASH!

SPLASH!

Wow!

The iceberg you see above water is just a small part of the whole thing. Most of the heavy iceberg floats under the water. Right, Mr. Whale?

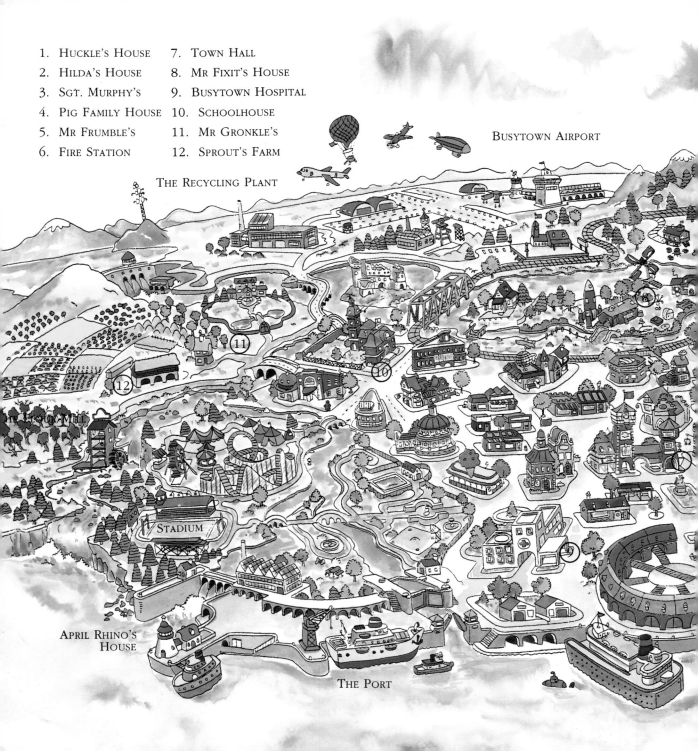

1. HUCKLE'S HOUSE
2. HILDA'S HOUSE
3. SGT. MURPHY'S
4. PIG FAMILY HOUSE
5. MR FRUMBLE'S
6. FIRE STATION
7. TOWN HALL
8. MR FIXIT'S HOUSE
9. BUSYTOWN HOSPITAL
10. SCHOOLHOUSE
11. MR GRONKLE'S
12. SPROUT'S FARM

BUSYTOWN AIRPORT

THE RECYCLING PLANT

STADIUM

APRIL RHINO'S
HOUSE

THE PORT